Good Boy, Buddy

by Karen Walberg • illustrated by John Speirs

Ana took Buddy to the store.

"Be a good boy," said Ana.

Ana went into the store.

But Buddy was not a good boy. Buddy saw a squirrel. He had to chase the squirrel!

The squirrel ran into the park.

Buddy ran into the park, too.

The squirrel climbed a tree. Buddy could not climb the tree. Buddy wanted the squirrel to come down. But the squirrel did not come down.

Then Buddy saw a butterfly.

He had to chase the butterfly!

Buddy chased the butterfly
over a bridge. Buddy wanted
the butterfly to come back.

But the butterfly did not come back.

Then Buddy saw a boy on a bike.
Buddy had to chase the boy!

Buddy chased the boy
over the bridge.

Buddy and the boy went out of the park.

They went back to the store.

Ana came out of the store.

She saw Buddy.

"Good boy, Buddy,"
she said.